CONTENTS

WHAT ARE STARS?

Stars are large balls of burning gas. They are formed when large clouds of dust and gas gather together. When a star burns gas, it gives off massive amounts of heat and light. This is what makes stars twinkle and allows us to see them in the night sky, even though they are millions of miles away. Some stars burn hotter than others. Very hot stars look white or blue, while cooler ones look red or orange.

Did you know that our Sun is a star? Every second it burns 5 billion kilogrammes of gas. This gives us the light in our sky and the heat we need to keep our planet warm enough to support life. Without the Sun we would not be here today.

Stars are much bigger than planets. In fact, the Sun is 100 times larger than Earth! The Sun is a medium-sized star, meaning there are some stars that are much bigger. Antares, one of the largest stars in the galaxy, is over 680 times as large as the Sun! Imagine how much heat it must give off!

STARGAZING

Why can't we see stars during the day? It's not because they go away. In fact, they are right where they were the night before, we just can't see them. This is because the Sun's light is so bright that it **blocks** out the other stars. At night when our planet is turned away from the Sun, the sky is dark, allowing us to see the other stars.

In large cities it can be difficult to see many stars at night because of 'light pollution'. Light pollution refers to the bright lights that buildings and street lights give off. **Rural** areas or places where there aren't many people, like the desert, are the best places to see the stars. In these places you can see more than 2000 individual stars each night! Have you ever seen the stars from a really dark place?

CONSTELLATIONS

Have you ever seen a plough in the night sky? Some stars are grouped together in such a way as to suggest a pattern or picture, often of a person, animal or everyday object. These patterns are called **constellations**. Humans have been naming constellations and creating stories about them since the beginning of time.

There are thousands of constellations. Some of the most widely known are: Leo (the lion), Canis Major (the great dog), Orion (the hunter), Scorpius (the scorpion) and Taurus (the bull).

Before there were maps, our **ancestors** used constellations to find their way at night. In fact, people used to travel across the seas on boats using only the Sun and the night sky as their guide!

CONSTELLATIONS

Different **cultures** have different names and stories for constellations. In North America, The Plough is called 'The Big Dipper' because it looks like a giant spoon! In some Middle Eastern cultures, Canis Major is seen as a bow and arrow not a dog. Over time, constellations can change in size and shape or disappear entirely.

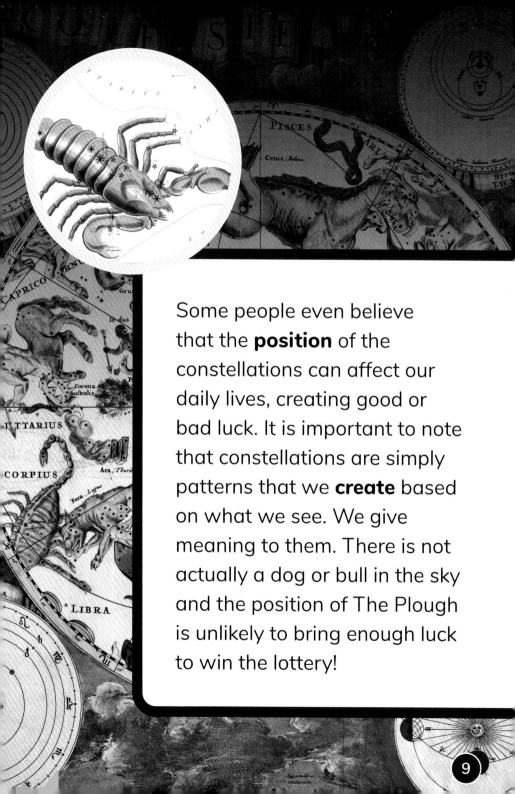

Some people even believe that the **position** of the constellations can affect our daily lives, creating good or bad luck. It is important to note that constellations are simply patterns that we **create** based on what we see. We give meaning to them. There is not actually a dog or bull in the sky and the position of The Plough is unlikely to bring enough luck to win the lottery!

THE DEATH OF A STAR

Most stars will shine bright for billions of years. Our Sun is over 4 billion years old, and it will continue to burn for another 5 billion years. As stars get older, though, they begin to run out of gas. A star dies when it no longer has enough gas left to burn. How a star ends its life will depend on how big it is.

If the star is really big, like Antares, it will eventually **explode** in a spectacular display called a supernova. This explosion will scatter the star's remaining gas and dust into the **galaxy** to form the beginnings of new stars.

Luckily, we don't have to worry about our Sun exploding. Medium to small sized stars like the Sun don't explode. Instead, they grow bigger before slowly cooling off and shedding their outer layers, leaving behind a small core called a 'white dwarf'. Almost all of the stars in our galaxy are or will become white dwarfs.

GLOSSARY

stargazing: identifying stars and planets in the night sky

blocks: stops light from passing through something

rural: the countryside

constellations: clusters of stars that create imaginary shapes

ancestors: people who were in someone's family in past times

cultures: particular groups of people

position: the place where something is

create: to make something new, or invent something

explode: a sudden and often violent burst of energy

galaxy: a large group of stars and planets held together by gravity

The definition given is the meaning of the word as it is used in the book.